9/91

CRITTERLAN

OCEAN FISH
SCHOOL

Story and pictures by Bob Reese

CHILDRENS PRESS, CHICAGO

MY 35 WORDS ARE:

The	to	you
oyster	learn	teach
whale	about	us
pelican	sea	makes
too	rocks	a
sponge	sand	pearl
lobster	seaweed	for
greenfish	octopus	me
and	said	snorkeling
blue	we	diving
they	can	but
came	from	

Library of Congress Cataloging in Publication Data
Reese, Bob.
 Ocean fish school.
 (Critterland adventures)
 Summary: Each of the various inhabitants of
the ocean has a special skill to demonstrate.
 [1. Marine animals—Fiction. 2. Stories in
rhyme] I. Title. II. Series.
PZ8.3.R2550c 1983 [E] 82-23572
ISBN 0-516-02314-4 AACR2

OYSTER
ISLAND

SNORKEL
BAY

CORAL
REEF

SPONGEE
SPONGE
LAND

PELICAN
ISLAND

LOBSTER
ISLAND

OCTOPUS
ISLAND

WHALE
ISLAND

The oyster,

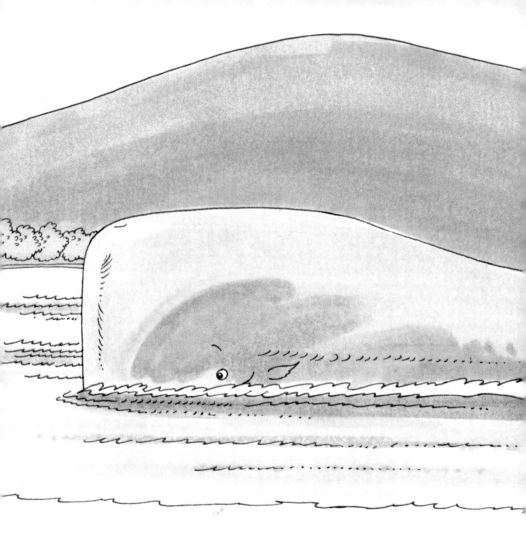

the whale,

the pelican too.

The sponge,

the lobster,

greenfish and blue.

They came to learn
about the sea,

about rocks,

about sand,

about seaweed.

The Octopus said,
"We can learn from you,

the oyster, the whale,
the pelican too.

The oyster can teach us
about the sea.

The oyster makes a pearl
for you and me.

The whale can teach us
about the sea.

The whale teaches snorkeling
to you and me.

The pelican can teach us
about the sea.

The pelican teaches diving
to you and me."

They came to learn
about the sea,

about rocks, about sand,
about seaweed.

But the Octopus said,
"We can learn from you,

the oyster, the whale,
the pelican too."